PALL BEARERS AND PEPPERONI

Papa Pacelli's Pizzeria Series, Book 1

PATTI BENNING

Summer Prescott Books Publishing

Chapter One

"Well, Bunny, we're here."

Eleanora Pacelli shut off her car's engine and unbuckled her seatbelt, which sent her little black-and-white papillon, Bunny, into a spinning frenzy in the passenger seat. After two nine-hour days spent on the road, she didn't blame the dog for being excited to have a chance to stretch her legs at last.

"Remember, be nice to Nonna. It was very nice of her to let you come, too, and I want you to be on your very best behavior."

The little dog's tail began wagging even faster at her owner's words, which Ellie decided to take as a sign of agreement. She grabbed a thin leather leash and clipped it to the ring on Bunny's harness before scooping the eight-pound dog into her arms and depositing her gently on the ground outside of the car. Bunny in the lead, the two of them approached the maroon front door, which opened before they reached the stoop. In the doorway stood a strong-boned elderly woman with curled white hair and wearing a pair of turquoise reading glasses from a cord around her neck.

"Ellie! My goodness, girl, you've grown since I've last seen you. I'd never forget that face, though."

Before she knew it, Ellie found herself enveloped in her grandmother's arms. With one hand clasping the leash and the other holding onto her purse, she returned the hug as best she could.

"Of course I've grown, Nonna," she said when they pulled apart. "It's been twenty-five years since we've seen each other."

Ann Pacelli was her paternal grandmother, and after Ellie's father had washed his hands of her and her mother, they had fallen out of touch with his side of the family. Oh, sure, she still got the yearly birthday call from her grandma, but she and her mother hadn't actually made the trip out here to visit since the divorce. It was a source of guilt for Ellie—she had had plenty of opportunity to visit on her own over the years, but had kept putting it off. Now, she had waited too long; her grandfather had passed away just weeks ago. She had never been close to the serious, quiet man, but had still been stunned to hear of his unexpected passing.

"Over twenty years," the old woman said, shaking her head slowly. "I can't believe it. It seems like just yesterday that you were a tiny little girl begging me to take her down to the ocean."

"It's crazy how quickly time passes," Ellie agreed. A high-pitched yap brought her attention down to the papillon, who was standing on her hind legs between them in an effort to draw attention to herself. "Oh, this is Bunny, my dog."

"Bunny? I thought I must have heard you wrong on the phone." Ann bent down, a careful hand kept on the front stoop's railing for support, and petted the little dog, who gave her hand a flurry of kisses.

"We never planned to name her that, but her ears were so big when she was a puppy that Ken kept saying she looked like a little rabbit… and the name Bunny just sort of stuck."

She fell silent, trying to tamp down the emotion that flooded her whenever she thought of her fiancé. *Ex*-fiancé, she reminded herself. He had made the ex-part very clear when he moved in with his old girlfriend.

"Bunny… it's cute," her grandmother said,

straightening up. "I just hope she doesn't frighten Marlowe."

"Who's Marlowe? I thought it would just be you and me here."

"Why don't you come in and see?" The old woman asked with a mischievous twinkle in her eye. "I'll introduce you to Marlowe and give you the grand tour, then you can bring your bags in and start getting settled."

With a firm grip on Bunny's leash, she followed her nonna into the big white colonial house. She wasn't surprised to find that although she hadn't been inside the house since shortly after her sixteenth birthday, the interior was mostly just as she remembered. There was, however, one glaring difference. Next to the stairs in the front room was a huge birdcage, which held a giant red parrot with green and blue feathers on its wings.

"Ellie, this is Marlowe. Marlowe, meet Ellie."

The bird ruffled its feathers in a way that Ellie imagined wasn't totally friendly, although to be fair she knew about as much about birds as she knew about ancient Greek—not much at all.

"What is it?" she asked, taking a hesitant step toward the cage.

"She's a green-winged macaw," her grandmother

explained. "She belonged to your grandfather. He got her just after he opened the pizzeria. She's nineteen years old."

"Wow," Ellie said. "How long do they usually live?"

"I think your grandfather said that one of the oldest macaws in the world was confirmed to be over a hundred, although they don't all live that long. She'll outlive me, that's for sure."

"She's gorgeous. Hi, Marlowe. You're such a pretty—"

The bird lunged at the cage bars, making Ellie jump back and break off in the middle of her sentence.

"She hasn't let anyone get near her since Art died," her grandmother said with a chuckle. "I should have warned you. She used to live in his study, but since no one goes in there anymore, I thought she would be happier out here. Well, let's get started on that tour. We've changed some things since you were here last. After that, I'm sure you're eager to begin unpacking."

With a backwards glance at the angry red bird, Ellie followed her grandmother down the hall. She did her best to remember where everything was, but she was exhausted, and still reeling from the dual blow of losing her fiancé and her job in the same week. All she wanted was to curl up in bed with Bunny and sleep the rest of the day away.

Her wish was partially granted—after the tour, she lugged her bags upstairs and chose the largest of the three bedrooms on the upper level as hers. It was a corner room, with two big windows, an attached bathroom, and a sizable closet. Since her grandmother didn't go upstairs anymore, the entire upper level of the house was Ellie's to do with as she pleased. Still tired from her long drive, she put off unpacking and settled in for a nap.

She woke up a few hours later to the delicious scent of food in the air, and an eager papillon waiting by the bedroom door. Ellie glanced at her phone and realized, with a surge of guilt, that it was dinnertime. She had meant to help with the cooking; she was determined not to be a burden to her grandmother, who was in her late eighties. Although unusually active for her age, the elderly woman surely wouldn't appreciate any extra work that Ellie's presence caused her.

Her clothes were rumpled from the nap, so she hurried into the bathroom to change. Her straight dark hair, which had never been easy to style, was a mess. Her makeup was smudged, and her brown eyes—

which she had always thought of as boring and earthy —were slightly red and irritated from sleeping with her contacts in.

"I look terrible," she muttered. She turned on the faucet and splashed cold water on her face, determined to clean herself up a little bit before helping her grandmother finish making dinner.

Her grandmother, it turned out, did not need any help whatsoever. The kitchen was spotless, and on the table in the breakfast nook was a meal worthy of a magazine spread. Baked lobster tails still in the shell with small dishes of melted butter beside them for dipping, creamy mashed potatoes, corn on the cob, and a bean and mushroom casserole with lightly browned breadcrumbs on top.

"I was just about to come wake you," her grandmother said as Ellie took in the table. "I just finished dinner."

"Wow, Nonna, this looks delicious," Ellie breathed. "You should have woken me up. I would have helped."

"Nonsense, dear. It's your first day here. Tomorrow will be busy enough for you. This is the least I could do."

"Thank you. I can't wait to taste it."

The meal was every bit as scrumptious as it

looked. Ellie ate until she felt like she would burst. Even then, it was hard to resist taking a second serving. Her grandmother definitely was a good cook. The taste of the food brought her back to early childhood, but the memories were bittersweet, and she pushed them aside for the moment. There were more urgent matters to discuss.

"So… tomorrow," she began. "I… uh… I guess I still don't know exactly what you want me to do. I know you wanted help with finances, and I can do that, but running a pizzeria is a far cry from working as a financial consultant in Chicago."

"You can start by going through the papers in your grandfather's study. He kept handwritten records of everything he put into his restaurant—Art never did trust computers. The pizzeria doesn't open until noon, so that should give you time to get some idea of what state your grandfather left things in. I told Xavier that you would be stopping by at some point tomorrow, so he should be expecting you."

"Xavier… he's the manager, right?"

"Assistant manager," her grandmother corrected. "He's been there for two years, and he should know the ropes enough to show you around and introduce you to the other employees."

"And, well, what will my job be, exactly?"

"You're taking over for your grandfather, sweetie. You'll be the boss, so you can be just as involved as you'd like to be. I don't know the first thing about your grandfather's plans for the pizzeria, all I want is for it to stay open. It was his darling, you understand. I just don't have the energy to try to manage it. Any profit you turn over from it is yours to keep—I have more than enough from his pension and our savings."

"I can get a head start on his records tonight if you'd like," Ellie said. The thought of being responsible for the business that her grandfather had spent over thirty years building made her stomach roil with anxiety; going through the financial records would at least take her mind off of the monumental job ahead of her. She was plagued by doubt once again—had she made a mistake in coming here and agreeing to help her grandmother? Would it have been better to stay in Chicago and try to find another job there, one that she was actually qualified for?

It's too late to change my mind now, she told herself. *If this doesn't work out, I can always leave after a few months. I just have to help Nonna get back on her feet first. Losing Papa has been hard on her.*

"If you'd like, dear, go ahead. I'll fetch you the key to his study before I head off to bed. I've got an early doctor's appointment, so I'll be gone when you wake up, but I'll have my mobile phone with me, so you feel free to call me if you have any questions—or if Xavier gives you any trouble. From the little I've heard about him from your grandfather, he can be quite the character."

What's that supposed to mean? Ellie thought, feeling momentary panic. *Am I going to have trouble with the employees right off the bat? Was this move really the right thing to do? Maybe I should have tried to pick up the pieces back in Chicago after all.* Even if she had made the wrong choice, it was too late to pack up and go home. She would just have to see what the next day brought.

Chapter Two

Ellie woke up the next morning to an empty house and a feeling of dread in the pit of her stomach. Going over her grandfather's finances for the pizzeria hadn't put her at ease as she had hoped. Instead, it had driven home the dire reality of the situation in which Arthur Pacelli had left his business. The pizzeria had been losing money for the last two years. Her grandfather had reached into his own pocket quite a few times just to keep the place running.

If this was something a client showed me, I would suggest that they cut their losses and sell the place, she thought. *But I don't have that option. I promised Nonna that I would keep the restaurant open; in exchange, she's giving me the chance to have a fresh start here after the mess I made of my life in Chicago.*

Ellie didn't have the faintest idea how she was going to keep that promise, but she was prepared to try... although she knew it wouldn't be easy by a long shot.

"I guess I'll just have to try to stay optimistic and face the day, Bunny," she said to the little dog, who was curled up on the pillow next to her. At the sound of her name, the papillon's oversized ears perked up. Ellie smiled. "I know just the thing to start with. Do you want to go outside?"

At those words the dog leapt off the bed and rushed over to the bedroom door. She began spinning in excited circles as she waited for her owner to drag herself out of bed.

"At least one of us is enthusiastic about starting the day," Ellie said. "Now, where did I put your leash?"

The morning was chilly and grey, a far cry from the eighty-degree weather she had left behind in Chicago. She remembered the summers that she had spent here as a child; they might be in for another hot and toasty day or two, but by the end of the month the average temperature would have dropped down to the sixties. *Guess I won't be wearing these for much longer,* she thought, looking down at her sandals. Before she knew it, she would have to bundle up for the Northeast winter.

While she waited for Bunny to do her business, she looked around. The area around her grandparents' big colonial house, just north of the small town of Kittiport, had changed substantially in the twenty-five years since she last visited—a few more houses had popped up, and the road was paved with fresh blacktop instead of gravel—but the area was still far from being urban. She could see the steely grey line of the ocean over the hill across the road, and when the breeze gusted she thought she could even smell the distinctive scent of the salty waves. Her grand-mother's yard backed up to a pine forest that was part of a state park. Ellie, used to living in a little apart-ment in downtown Chicago, loved the thought of having wilderness right outside her door.

"All set?" she asked when the little dog came prancing up to her. She realized that Bunny probably didn't even need the leash—they didn't exactly live in a busy city anymore. This move was going to be a big change for both of them, but there were definitely some bright spots.

Inside she found a basket of freshly baked blue-berry muffins waiting for her on the table in the breakfast nook, along with a handwritten note.

Ellie, would you be a dear and feed Marlowe for me? Her food is in the pantry. She might also appre-

ciate a bite of one of these muffins. I'll see you this evening. I can't wait to hear all about your first day at the pizzeria!

After reading through the note, she put it down and reluctantly got up to look in the pantry for the bird's food. While she feared Marlowe's giant beak, but she couldn't very well let the poor thing starve.

She found a bag of colorful pellets with a picture of a macaw on the front and filled the scoop inside with the food. After hesitating a second, she broke off a sizable chunk of muffin. If she was going to approach the bird, it was probably best to do it with a bribe.

Marlowe eyed her warily as she walked toward the cage. *She really is a beautiful bird*, Ellie thought. *It's a pity she's so unfriendly. Even Nonna can't hold her.* She knew the bird hadn't always been this way; when she was in her grandfather's study the evening before going over his files for the pizzeria, she had seen pictures of him with Marlowe. The two of them seemed to have been inseparable.

"Do you miss Papa?" she asked quietly, peering into the cage at the bird. "Is that why you're so upset? Do you somehow know that he isn't coming back? I don't know much about macaws, but I think you're supposed to be pretty smart."

She was relieved to see that the food and water dishes were mounted on little doors that could swing out of the cage. At least she wouldn't have to reach her entire arm inside the cage; she was certain to get bit if she tried that. As it was, she still jumped back when the bird lunged at her from inside the bars. That beak was just so *big*.

"Look, I just want to feed you, all right? I'm not trying to invade your personal space. I even have a piece of blueberry muffin for you..." She held up the chunk of muffin, which the bird seemed to recognize. Marlowe climbed back up to her perch and began bobbing her head up and down, her eyes on the muffin all the while.

"I'm guessing that means you'll let me put the food in your dish?" Ellie asked. "Just don't try to bite me, okay?"

Moving slowly, she opened the little door by the food dish and dumped the colorful pellets into the dish. Watching the bird closely, she placed the chunk of muffin on top, then shut the door. In a flash, the bird climbed down to the food dish and began eating the blueberry muffin.

"Well, that's one challenge done and over with for the day," Ellie told the bird, stepping back and wiping her palms on her tee shirt. "Time to focus on the next one—saving my grandfather's business."

Ellie drove slowly by the old building that housed her grandfather's pizzeria. A neon sign with the lettering *Pa a Pace li's Piz ria* glowed in the window. The burned-out letters gave the place a run-down, disreputable look.

"It could be worse," she muttered to herself as she turned her blinker on and rounded the corner, looking for the entrance to the parking lot behind the building. "This place *used* to turn a profit, after all. With any luck, it will be an easy fix and I can turn my attention to what's really important: finding a way to piece my career back together."

She parked her car next to a rusted silver pickup truck and started toward the building. The rear entrance was marked *Employees Only.* She hesitated, then squared her shoulders and pushed through the door. If she was in charge of the pizzeria now, she should act like it.

Chapter Three

"Watch out!"

A young man carrying a pizza box and wearing a black and red baseball cap with the restaurant's name embroidered on it narrowly missed running into her. She jumped back, stumbling into the legs of another employee—a blond girl sitting on the counter and chewing gum.

"Sorry!" Ellie exclaimed, flustered. Both employees were glaring at her. *Great start I've made,* she thought, upset with herself.

"Didn't you see the sign, lady? It says this entrance is for employees only. Guests are supposed to go around front." This was from another young man, one who looked slightly older than the other two. He had curly black hair, and a pin on his shirt that designated him as the manager.

"You must be Xavier," Ellie said, straightening up and trying to gather herself. She hadn't made a good first impression, but maybe that could still be salvaged. "I'm Eleanora Pacelli. I believe my grand-mother spoke to you. She's given me the pizzeria. I'm your new boss."

The silence in the kitchen was deafening. She watched closely as a myriad of emotions flick-ered across the manager's face; surprise, annoy-ance, maybe even anger. At last his expression settled into a simpering smile that didn't touch his eyes.

"Ah, Miss Pacelli. I think Ann did mention some-thing about you stopping by today. It's nice to meet you. I'm Xavier Hurst."

He stuck out a greasy hand, which Ellie shook reluctantly. She already disliked the young man, and would have bet money that he felt the same way toward her.

"I'm Rose Oliver," the girl said, sliding off the counter. "And the guy that ran into you is Jacob Stevens."

Ellie looked around. Jacob seemed to have vanished.

"He was on his way out for a delivery," Rose added, snapping her gum. "He'll be back in a bit."

"Oh. Well, it's very nice to meet all of you," Ellie said. "Um, let's get started then, shall we?" She turned to Xavier, who stared at her.

"Started with what?" he asked.

"I'm here to turn this place around and do what I can to figure out why it's losing money," she explained. "Didn't my grandmother tell you that?" Was she imagining it, or had he paled?

"Uh, I guess. I kinda thought you'd want me to handle everything, like I have been. Arthur sort of let me have free rein."

It took Ellie a second to realize that he meant her grandfather. She frowned. "Well, I plan on doing things a little bit differently than he did. I know this place was a hobby for him, but to me, it's a business. My grandmother and I can't afford to be losing money on it. Today I'll just observe and see if I notice anything that can be fixed right away. I'll keep going over the finances this week, and do my best to figure out exactly what's going wrong. Papa Pacelli's used to be the most popular pizzeria in town. I want to see it back at the top within the year."

She ignored the wide-eyed glance that Xavier and

Rose exchanged and took out her tablet, already making a list of things to fix before the week was out.

By the time she was done assessing just the physical state of the restaurant, she had a frighteningly long list. From the semi-working neon sign out front to the greasy stoves in the back, it was evident that Papa Pacelli's really needed a good, thorough cleaning. Beneath all of the grime, it was a nice-looking place. The walls in the dining area weren't painted, but rather covered with black and red tiles the size of dessert plates. The floor was a dark, natural hardwood that would glow with a good cleaning. There were four booths and two tables; ample room for guests to sit in and eat, although few chose to do so. The appliances in the kitchen were all good quality, if a bit old. With some tender, loving care, the pizzeria was sure to become a popular eatery once again.

Tired of looking at dusty shelves and walls with pizza sauce stains, she decided to spend the last part of the day observing how the employees interacted with the customers. She already suspected that a large part of the reason for the restaurant's losing money was from indifferent customer service. No one wanted to eat at a restaurant where the service wasn't good. Good service was almost as important as the quality of the food, and what she saw in the first few minutes alone did not impress her.

"Rose, why are three of the tables still covered in dishes from guests that left half an hour ago?" Ellie asked.

"Cleaning the tables is Jacob's job," the girl told her. "He's out on a delivery."

"He left for his last delivery two hours ago. He isn't back yet?"

The blonde woman shook her head. "I guess I can clean the tables off if you want, though. Give me a shout if someone else comes in, 'kay?"

Ellie watched the young employee begin stacking plates at the nearest table. She was fuming. It was obvious that the main issue that was holding back the pizzeria's success was the employees' poor work ethic. She had originally accepted the job of turning the pizzeria's finances around because it was important to her grandmother, but now the project felt more personal. This was her family's restaurant—the employees had no right to treat it the way that they did.

Her mental tirade was interrupted by the cheery jingling of the bell on the front door as a customer walked in. She turned to face him, but the words

"Welcome to Papa Pacelli's" faltered on her lips. His was a face that she would have recognized anywhere.

"Ben Elkton?" she said, her eyes widening with surprise. He stared at her for a moment before a wide grin broke across his face.

"Eleanora? Is that really you? Little Ellie Pacelli?"

Ellie winced. She had always hated being called that in school. At the start of every year she had tried to insist that her teachers and friends a call her by her full name, Eleanora, but despite her efforts, "Ellie Pacelli" had stuck. One of the many things that she had been looking forward to about marriage was the fact that she would, at last, have a different name. One that didn't rhyme. *Just another dream down the drain*, she thought, letting the familiar bitterness flood her for a moment before she shook her head and focused on the man in front of her.

Ben Elkton had been her high school sweetheart, and seeing him brought back long-forgotten memories in a rush. He looked as handsome as ever, with his neatly trimmed black hair, just starting to go grey around the edges, mischievous hazel eyes, and a slightly crooked nose. She remembered the day it got broken, during a fight with his cousin.

"It's really me." Her face split into a grin to match

his. "I can't believe you're still here. I thought you always wanted to move out west?"

"It's still a dream of mine, but life got in the way," he said with a shrug. "My old man got sick just before I left for college, and I had to take over the business while he saw specialists. I'll get out of this town someday, though. No, what I'm really surprised about is seeing you here. It's been what, twenty years?"

"About that. I'm back for the foreseeable future, though. I'm sure you heard about my grandfather?"

He nodded. "I'm very sorry about his passing. He was a good man. Are you staying with your grandmother now?"

"I am. She's lonely in that big house without him, and I was ready for a change of career, so it's working out well for both of us." She wasn't quite ready to tell him about her failed relationship and the mess that she had made of her previous job; thankfully, he didn't ask her any more about it.

"That's very kind of you. I'm sure she appreciates it." He hesitated, then cleared his throat and added, "Say, do you want to get dinner tonight? I'd love the chance to catch up more. It's not often that you run into old friends."

"Sure," Ellie said. "Just tell me when and where, and I'll be there."

She fought hard to keep from smiling like an idiot. It seemed that she was still just as vulnerable to Ben's charms as ever. *Don't get ahead of yourself,* she thought. *He's probably happily married. He did say that this would be a chance to catch up... as friends.*

"What do you say about the Lobster Pot at eight?" he asked.

"That place is still open? I'll be there. It was nice to run into you, Ben," she said.

"You, too." He smiled at her. "I'll see you tonight."

He made to leave, then turned back around with a foolish grin on his face. "I almost forgot to pick up my order. I should have a Hawaiian back there somewhere."

"Just a second, I'll check."

After he left with his pizza, Rose, who had finished clearing off the tables, came over with a smirk on her face. "Looks like you've got a date."

"It's not a date... just dinner, as friends," Ellie objected. The young woman chuckled and, shaking her head, began wiping down the counter with a wrung-out rag.

Chapter Four

The Lobster Pot had been one of the most popular restaurants in town for as long as Ellie could remember. When she used to live in Kittiport, she and her parents would eat there a few times each month. It didn't seem to have changed much from what she remembered.

"Well, here goes," she said once she parked her vehicle. She flipped down the visor and looked at herself in the mirror. Had she gone too far with the makeup? She kept telling herself that this wasn't a date, but she had been unable to resist the opportunity to gussy up a little for Ben. Her eyeshadow was dark and smoky, and her lipstick was an alluring red. Her hair, straight and boring as ever, was pulled back in a messy bun, held back by her nicest hair clip. She was wearing black dress pants and a blue blouse with a gold camisole underneath.

At least I don't look *like I was just cheated on by my fiancé and fired from my job*, she thought. *I don't look bad at all, really.* She gave herself an encouraging smile in the mirror, then shut the visor. It was time to find Ben and officially start their not-a-date dinner.

"I still can't believe it," Ben said, shaking his head. "Ellie Pacelli. I never thought I'd see you again after you and your mom moved to Illinois when we were in high school."

They were seated at a booth near the back of the restaurant, next to a window that looked out over the marina. Ben was sipping a beer, and Ellie was nursing a glass of chardonnay. It felt good to relax and enjoy being back after being so stressed about the pizzeria all day.

"I should have visited," she said. "I feel bad about that. I missed out on the last chance to see my grandfather before he died, and I don't know if I'll ever be able to forgive myself for that."

"Don't be hard on yourself," he said, settling his hand over hers. "From what I heard, his death was unexpected. There was no way you could have known you'd have so little time left."

Ellie looked down at their hands and felt a flutter in her stomach. After leaving Kenneth, she hadn't even considered dating another man. But maybe her future wouldn't be as bleak and lonely as she had thought.

"Oh—I'm sorry," Ben said, following her gaze to their hands. He pulled his back with a jerk. "I didn't mean to… you're probably married…"

He broke off, coughing awkwardly and taking another swallow of beer. Ellie grinned, finding his embarrassment endearing.

"I'm not married," she assured him. "I thought you might be, though."

"Nope." He grimaced. "Divorced. Going on five years now. I've got one son, but he lives with her."

"I'm sorry," she said.

"It's all right. I've got the furniture shop to keep me busy, and I get to see Josh on the weekends. He and his mom moved down to Portland. I think he likes the bigger city better anyway. Let's talk about you. How long do you think you'll be here?"

"I honestly don't know," Ellie said. "Don't tell anyone I told you this, but Papa Pacelli's hasn't been doing so well. It's actually losing money right now, and while my grandmother wants to keep it open, she can't do it for much longer if things don't turn around. So I suppose I'll see if I can get the restaurant back on its feet. After that... I have no idea."

"Well, I hope you end up staying here for good this time," he said with a smile. "I'm looking forward to getting to know you again, Ellie Pacelli."

Their conversation trailed off after the waiter brought them their food. Both of them had ordered lobster—the Lobster Pot's specialty, after all. Lobster season was in full swing, and the delicious crustaceans had been caught just hours before.

Ellie had ordered baked lobster tail with Cajun seasoning, and a side of creamy lobster bisque. The soup was creamy and rich, and won her over immediately. She was glad the Lobster Pot had a take-out service as well—she imagined that she would be stopping here a lot after work to grab a couple of bowls of that bisque for dinner.

She was just finishing her last bite of lobster tail when the waiter reappeared to see if they would be wanting dessert. Ben glanced at her questioningly, and she shook her head.

"No thanks. I'm pretty full," she said.

The waiter handed them their check, which Ben insisted on paying for despite her protests.

"What sort of date would I be if I didn't pay?" he

asked. "If you feel like you have to, you can make up for it with a free pizza sometime."

"Oh, all right," she said, laughing. "I think I can make that happen."

They walked out to their cars side by side. Ellie felt happier than she had in a long time. She had always liked Ben. Even when they were teenagers, he had always been a genuinely good person. Their dinner together felt like the beginning of a whole new part of her life; her high-stress job and cheating fiancé seemed a world away back in Chicago.

"When are you free for another dinner?" he asked when they reached her car. "There's this wonderful new restaurant called the White Pine Kitchen a few miles outside of town. I'd love to take you there sometime."

"This week will be pretty busy while I get the pizzeria fixed up," she said. "I'm planning on going in before the restaurant opens tomorrow to get some cleaning done, and I'm sure I'll end up staying after it closes most days, too. I'm taking the weekend off, though, so how about Saturday?"

"I've got a poker game Saturday evening," he told her. He gave a sheepish smile. "Normally I'd cancel, but I won a bunch of money from one of the guys last time we played, and he's supposed to pay up this time. It might seem sort of dumb, but I'd like to be there. How about Sunday?"

"Sure," she said, chuckling. "Saturday night's poker night. I'll keep that in mind."

"I had a really nice time tonight, Ellie," he said, his tone becoming more serious. "I'm glad you came back."

"Me, too," she said softly. With some surprise, she realized that it was true. She had missed this town.

Their gazes met and held. It was a breathless moment that seemed to last an eternity before Ben kissed her on the cheek. It was a sweet kiss, and a second later he had pulled back and was wishing her a good night, leaving Ellie flustered as she got into her car and began the short drive home.

Sleep didn't come easily that night, despite her exhaustion from the long day at the pizzeria. It wasn't until late that she managed to doze off, with Bunny curled up by her head. She woke up later than she meant to the next morning, and hurried out the door after a rushed promise to tell her grandmother all about her date later that evening.

"I've got to get to the pizzeria and start tackling my to-do list," she explained. "I want to get some of it done before the employees show up, so I can show them what a difference some cleaning makes."

"All right, dear, but it's not good to skip breakfast. Won't you at least take a muffin to go with you?"

"No time," Ellie called back, one foot out the door. "I'll just grab a slice of pizza at work or something."

She hurried to the store to buy all of the supplies that she thought she'd need. On her way to the pizzeria, she called a repair company for the broken neon sign in the front window and arranged to have it picked up that evening. It felt good to be making progress, even if it was only a few small things. By the end of the week the pizzeria would be squeaky clean. Then she could start focusing on other things— like improving the employees' work ethic.

Just one small step at a time, she told herself as she got out of the car and started toward the pizzeria's employee entrance. *In no time at all, Papa Pacelli's will be a place where people actually* want *to eat.*

Her steps faltered as she neared the back entrance when she saw someone sitting, slouched, against the door. Kittiport didn't have much of a homeless population as far as she knew, but there *was* a bar just a block away. Had someone passed out here, drunk, the night before and slept most of the day away?

"Excuse me," she called, approaching the figure

cautiously. "Is everything okay? This is a business; you really shouldn't be—"

She broke off when she spotted the blood spatter on the brick wall behind the figure. She took one more hesitant step closer, leaning down to look at his face, certain that she recognized something about the person.

When she saw the open, blank hazel eyes, and the dark red stain on the front of his button-down shirt, she dropped her armful of cleaning chemicals and stumbled backwards, screaming. It was Ben, and he was very, very dead.

Chapter Five

"Calm down, ma'am, I just need you to go over your date with me one more time," asked the sheriff, a man about her age, with short brown hair and the tanned skin of someone who spent a lot of time outdoors. He tapped his notepad with his pen then frowned, rubbing his hand across his beard and mustache as he thought. "You said you last saw him at about eleven o'clock last night?"

"Yes." Ellie sniffed, wiping her nose with a tissue that a younger female deputy had given her. "We said goodbye at my car, then he left and I drove straight home."

She was a mess, and she knew it, but she couldn't seem to care. Her brain kept replaying the image of Ben's lifeless body slouched against the pizzeria's back door. She had already called everyone scheduled to work today and told them to take the day off. The restaurant was crawling with police and forensic teams, and there was no way they would be able to open.

"Did he say anything during your meal to make you think he was in fear for his life? Did he mention being in trouble with anyone, or owing anyone money?"

"No, he seemed happy." She took a deep, shuddering breath. "Ben was always a nice guy. This was the first time I've seen him in years, but I can't imagine that he would have changed that much. He never had any enemies. I can't imagine someone wanting to kill him."

"Exactly how long have you known Mr. Elkton?" he asked. A frown creased his forehead. "I don't think I've seen you around before."

"We were friends when we were kids, and dated for a while in high school," she explained. "I used to live here, but moved away in my junior year. Last night was the first time we'd seen each other in over twenty years."

She realized with a chill that she was the stranger here. Everyone else at the crime scene seemed to know each other. The young deputy who had given her the tissues was chatting casually with a member of the forensics team. Another deputy was on his way over to the table where she and the sheriff were sitting, and greeted the sheriff by name.

"Russ, we're taking the body to the coroner's office. Is there anything you need before I go?"

"No, I think I'm about done here, Liam. I'll join you shortly."

"All right. Oh, Bethany found these crushed underneath the body." The deputy put a pair of Polaroid photos on the table in front of Russ. "They've been taken in as evidence, but I thought you might want to ask Ms. Pacelli if she knows anything about them."

The sheriff looked down at the photo, then slid it across the table to Ellie as his friend walked away. "Any idea why Ben would be hanging around outside the pizzeria with flowers? Did you have plans to meet here this morning?"

She looked down at the photos and felt her breath catch as another wave of shock and grief washed over her. One of the photos was of a beautiful red rose, the petals crushed and falling off. The other was a note: *I had a really nice time. I can't wait for Sunday.*

"No. He… he knew I was going to come in before anyone else to clean. He must have been planning to leave them for me as a surprise." She gazed out the window. It was a deceptively beautiful day. The ocean was just visible down the street, with the sun glinting off the gently rolling waves. None of it felt real. Was it possible that she was still sleeping, and all of this was some kind of terrible nightmare?

"What was supposed to happen Sunday?" the sheriff asked, jolting her back to reality.

"We had another date planned," she told him.

He nodded and made a note with his pen. "Well, I think that's all for now. Here's my card, Ms. Pacelli. If you remember anything else, please don't hesitate to give me a call. I mean it; day or night. I want to get this crime solved. People just don't get murdered in Kittiport, and Ben was a friend. I'm taking this one personally."

His eyes, a stormy grey, glinted with cold determination as he handed her his card. She glanced down to read it. *Russell Ward, Sheriff.* When she looked up, he was gone.

Ellie hung around the pizzeria talking to the young female deputy, who introduced herself as Bethany, while the forensics team finished up with their work. She learned that Bethany had just been hired on as a deputy two weeks before, although she had dreamed of working in law enforcement her whole life.

"I'm terrified of making a mistake," she admitted once they got to talking.

"I know the feeling," Ellie said. "At least you have had the training you need to do your job well. I don't know the first thing about running a pizza place."

She was glad for the conversation. It kept her from thinking of the gruesome scene behind the pizzeria. She wasn't sure what she was going to do with the rest of the day—somehow she didn't think she would feel like scrubbing grease off the stoves with Ben's death still so fresh in her mind—but it didn't feel right to leave the pizzeria in the care of strangers.

"I used to love this place," Bethany mused quietly, startling Ellie, who had been eyeballing some dust bunnies behind the soda fridge.

"Really?" she asked. The other woman nodded.

"My friends and I came here to eat a couple times a week after school. Of course, that was years ago, before it started going downhill." She blushed, and backpedaled quickly. "I just meant… well…"

"I know what you mean," Ellie assured her. "I never actually saw this place when it was doing well, but I know that things really started going downhill about two years ago when my grandfather officially retired from managing it. I'm hoping to fix it up while I'm here."

"I hope you succeed," Bethany said earnestly. "It's always sad to see old businesses like this fall into disrepair. At least the pizza is still good, when it isn't already cold by the time it gets to my door, that is."

Ellie frowned. She would definitely have to tighten things up when it came to the pizzeria's employees. In such a small town as Kittiport, there was absolutely no excuse for pizzas to get delivered cold.

"I hope you'll give this place another chance, once I've made some changes," she said to the deputy.

"Oh, I will," the other woman assured her. "And I think you'll find that a lot of people remember Papa Pacelli's fondly, especially those of us that grew up with it being the best pizza place in town. You'll have plenty of support from us locals."

Ellie winced, but quickly covered it up with a smile. She wanted to point out that she was a local too —she had grown up just down the street, after all. But she knew that after having been gone for over half her life, it would take a while for the residents of Kittiport

Chapter Six

Ellie spent the rest of the day at home helping her grandmother rearrange the kitchen and occasionally depositing a treat in Marlowe's cage in an effort to befriend the intimidating bird. Bunny trailed along behind her wherever she went, seeming to sense that her owner was emotionally fragile.

While she would have liked to continue her moping the next day, she knew that the pizzeria wasn't going to clean itself. The sign repairers had picked up the neon sign the evening before, but that was only one small thing on the list of improvements she had planned to make that week.

"At least scrubbing the walls should take my mind off of poor Ben," she sighed as she parked her car behind the pizzeria. She was relieved to see that there were no bodies waiting for her at the door this morning. Finding Ben's body had shocked her deeply, and she didn't know if she would ever really get over it. It had been the worst experience of her life, and she had had a very bad year.

With only an hour before Xavier arrived to open the pizzeria, Ellie got to work. She began by sweeping and mopping both the kitchen and dining room floors, spending extra time waxing the wood flooring until it shone. The cleaning solution left a crisp, clean citrus scent in the air, which was indisputably better than the stale, greasy smell the place had had before.

By the time she had finished with the floors, Xavier had arrived, along with another employee whom Ellie hadn't met yet. The young woman with bushy brown hair and startlingly green eyes introduced herself as Clara.

"It's nice to meet you, Miss Pacelli," she said, giving the older woman an enthusiastic handshake. "It's cool that you're taking over the store."

Ellie grinned, an expression that faded when she saw Xavier's face. He was glaring at them angrily, and when he saw her looking at him he turned and stomped back into the kitchen. Clara followed her gaze with a worried expression.

"He's been in a bad mood ever since Ann—your grandmother, sorry, she told us to call her by her first name—spoke to us about you taking over the business," she explained. "I think he's just upset that he won't get to be the head honcho anymore. Your grandfather just sort of let him do his own thing once he hired him."

"I'm starting to realize that," Ellie said. "He doesn't seem to like me very much."

"Oh, he'll come around. You seem perfectly nice to me." Clara beamed at her. "Now, do you need any help? Xavier's on cooking duty today, so I don't have anything to do until someone comes in or we get an order for delivery."

"Sure. Grab a spray bottle and some paper towels and start cleaning off the tables, booths, and chairs. Some of them are a bit sticky. I'm going to get to work on cleaning the walls and getting the cobwebs out of the corners. If you get done with the tables before we get a customer, I'd appreciate some help in dusting off the light fixtures and vents."

Between the two of them they managed to scrub nearly every inch of the dining room before Ellie decided to call it a day. The eating area, which had been grungy the day before, now shone.

"Wow," Clara said in an impressed tone. "It looks

almost brand-new. I don't think the dining area has ever been this clean since I started working here."

"Well, let's try to keep it this way," Ellie said. "It should be a lot easier to maintain now that we've got it looking good. I'm sure we'll end up getting more sit-down customers too, since they'll have a clean place to sit for once."

The two of them retreated to the kitchen to wash up. Ellie's hands were raw from spending hours using harsh chemicals to clean. She had forgotten to buy gloves, and was paying for it now. She was also hungry, and realized she had no idea how to make herself food at the pizzeria.

"We usually share a pizza," Clara explained when she asked about it. "We each put whatever toppings we want on our portion, but you can also make a personal pizza if you want."

"I'm happy to share a pizza with you guys," Ellie said. "I want to help out and learn how everything works."

Xavier grudgingly showed her how they made the pizza dough. He poured the ingredients in an automatic mixer, then to her surprise went and got a ball of already-made pizza dough out of the fridge.

"We aren't going to use the fresh stuff?" she asked.

"You gotta let the dough sit in the fridge for a couple of days," he told her. "It cooks better that way. Whenever we use up any dough, we have to make more to replace it. The balls farthest to the left in the fridge are the newest, see?"

She peered into the fridge and nodded. It looked like she would have to do some research on how to cook pizza if she wanted to be able to run this restaurant well.

"What about sitting in the fridge makes the dough better?" she asked.

Xavier shrugged. "Something to do with the yeast or something. I just follow the instructions on the recipe."

He handed her a very old, laminated, yellow sheet of paper with a handwritten recipe. She recognized the handwriting from going through her grandfather's files in his study. The sight brought a smile to her face. She was about to eat a pizza made from the very same recipe that he had come up with all those years ago.

After Xavier kneaded and spun the blob of dough into a mostly round shape, he put it into one of the constantly running ovens and told Clara to get whatever toppings she wanted out of the fridge. When the pizza dough came out of the oven, looking much less like dough and more like a real pizza crust, the three of them spent a few minutes slathering it with sauce, and covering it with cheese and bits of onion, mushrooms, green peppers, and bacon. It went back in the oven to cook for a few more minutes, then at last their masterpiece was done.

"Oh my goodness," Ellie said, wiping a straggling string of cheese off her lip. "This is the best pizza I've ever had."

Clara chuckled, and Xavier just smirked. The three of them were sitting around a small table tucked into the back corner of the kitchen, with the pizza on a tray in front of them. Ellie grabbed a second piece before she even finished her first.

The cheese was melted and goopy, the crust was perfectly cooked and just bursting with flavor, and the sauce—which Ellie discovered was yet another original recipe of her grandfather's—was smooth and delicious, with the perfect amount of sweetness. Even though she burned her tongue on it more than once, Ellie couldn't stop herself from wolfing it down. *Papa Pacelli's has its fair share of problems*, she thought. *But the quality of food sure isn't one of them.*

She had just finished with her second piece and was trying to decide whether or not she would be able to finish a third when she heard the bell in the dining

44

room jingle, announcing the presence of a customer. Clara jumped up and waved a hand to indicate that the other two should continue eating. She hurried out of the kitchen—only to return a moment later.

"It's not a customer," she said. "It's someone wanting to talk to you, Ms. Pacelli."

Confused and curious, Ellie wiped her face and stood up. "Thanks for coming to get me, Clara. Feel free to sit back down and finish your meal."

She left the kitchen, wondering if the sheriff or one of his deputies had decided to stop by to ask her some more questions. Instead of a frowning official, she was confronted with a woman who gave a squeal of joy and hurried around the counter to envelop her in a crushing hug.

"Ellie! I couldn't believe my ears when James told me you were back."

"What—Shannon? I can't breathe—"

The other woman released her and took a step back, wearing an embarrassed grin. "Sorry. I'm just so excited to see you."

"It's nice to see you, too," Ellie said, returning the grin when she had finally caught her breath. She looked at the woman who had been her best friend growing up. Her friend had gained a few pounds, and her light brown hair was shorter now, but otherwise she looked almost the same as she always had. "You look good."

"Thanks. So do you. The way James was talking, I was expecting to find you a mess."

"Who's James?" Ellie asked.

"He's my husband, silly. I'm Shannon Ward now."

Ward. Ellie frowned, trying to figure out why the name sounded so familiar. Suddenly she remembered the sheriff's card. "Is he related to Russell Ward by any chance? The sheriff?"

"Yep. Russ is his brother. He's a great guy—came over for dinner last night like he does every week. I heard about Ben, by the way. It's terrible."

"Yes, it is," Ellie agreed. "Let's sit down. Do you want a slice of pizza? We have a lot to catch up on."

Chapter Seven

Reconnecting with her friend gave Ellie the boost that she needed to get through the week. Shannon stopped in the pizzeria almost every day to tell her a new story about some mutual friend they had known back in grade school, or bring her a pastry from one of the small shops around town. She was also Ellie's biggest cheerleader—more than any of the employees, she seemed to notice the daily improvement of the restaurant. With the neon sign repaired and the kitchen and dining area spic and span at last, Papa Pacelli's really did look like an entirely new restaurant by the time the weekend rolled around.

Ellie was glad for the time off, but was surprised to find that she wasn't dreading returning to the pizzeria on Monday. Besides spending her time cleaning, she had also learned how to make the pizzas and salads that the restaurant served, and was eager to try her hand at making a few pizzas herself. She already had an idea for a way to boost the employee morale during the week, and was planning on spending the next few days finessing it.

"I'm glad things are working out so well, dear," her grandmother said over breakfast on Saturday morning. "It seems like you have pizza in your blood. It must have skipped a generation."

The last part was muttered somewhat bitterly under her breath. Ellie knew Ann was talking about Ellie's father, her son Harvey. After the divorce, he had moved to Canada, doing his best to leave both his parents and Ellie and her mother in the past.

"I like fixing up Papa Pacelli's, Nonna," she said, pouring herself more juice. "I know Papa would be proud to see it now."

"I'm sure he would. I'll stop in later this week and look at all of the progress you've made." Her grandmother's eyes brightened. "Say, have you been down to the marina yet to see the *Eleanora?*"

"Huh?"

"Your grandfather's boat," the elderly woman explained, her eyes twinkling. "He bought after I convinced him his old one the *Hermit Crab* wasn't worth repairing anymore. He named it after you. Let's go to the marina this afternoon and take a look at it."

The Kittiport marina was bustling with activity when they got there. It was a beautiful Saturday, the perfect sort of day for a fishing trip or just going out on the water with a friend. Ellie followed her grandmother as she weaved between young couples, families with kids, and gruff old fishermen. The *Eleanora* was moored in a slip at the far end of the marina. She was a beautiful white boat, similar to the type that many lobster catchers used, but a bit more luxurious. The name, printed on the side in elegant, curving letters, made Ellie smile.

"You can get on if you want," her grandmother said. "I get horribly seasick, so I'll stay on solid ground. I never was a boat person."

Ellie stepped from the dock to the boat, taking a moment to steady herself as she got used to the bob and sway of the vessel. She walked around slowly, interested to see everything she could about the boat that was named after her. The cabin was small, but comfortable, and smelled of cigars. There were some high-tech screens by the wheel, but she had no idea what they did. She wondered what would happen to the boat, now that her grandfather was gone. She certainly wouldn't know how to take it out safely, and it would be a pity to let such a beautiful vessel spend all of its days sitting at the marina.

"What do you think?" Ann asked when Ellie returned to the dock.

"It's gorgeous. Thanks for showing it to me," she replied.

"You can take it out whenever you want."

"Thanks, Nonna. Maybe I'll take you up on that offer, when I'm less busy at the pizzeria." *And after I get some sailing lessons,* she thought. *Do you even call them sailing lessons if the boat doesn't have a sail? What would they be… boat driving lessons?*

"Ms. Pacelli?"

Hearing her name, Ellie spun around. The sheriff, Russell Ward, was standing a few feet away, looking surprised.

"I thought I recognized you. Gotta say, I didn't expect you to still be in town."

"Why would I leave?" Ellie asked, puzzled.

"Not many people would stick around if they didn't have to, not after a murder happened practically on their doorstep."

"Well, I—" She broke off. Saying she had nowhere else to go would sound too pathetic. She was nearly forty, for goodness sake. She wasn't about to admit that she had nothing more to show for her life than a tiny dog and a nice car. "The pizzeria is a family business; I wouldn't just walk out on it."

He nodded, and she thought she saw a flash of approval in his eyes. She realized for the first time that he was wearing casual clothing, and had a tackle box in his hand. He inclined his head toward a boat tied up on the other side of the dock.

"I'm about to head out with my buddy, Duncan," he said. "We're going to try our luck with the fish. You two have a nice day." He nodded to them and took a step toward his boat, then hesitated. "Say, you wouldn't happen to own a 9mm pistol, would you, Ms. Pacelli? Sorry to spring this on you now, but it'll save me a phone call when I'm back on duty."

He was talking to Ellie, but it was her grandmother that spoke up.

"I sure do, Sheriff. You know Art, he was always worried about leaving me home alone. He bought me one for our fifty-third anniversary."

Russell's eyes narrowed, and he swept his gaze over Ellie consideringly. She shifted on her feet, not sure where to look. His slate eyes seemed to pierce her. Did this have something to do with Ben's murder? It had to.

"Russ?" a voice called out. Ellie turned to see a muscular man around her own age with closely shaven dark hair and a camo fishing vest approaching them, a large cooler in tow. He gave her a curious look before turning to the sheriff. "You about ready to go? The fish're biting."

"Yeah, I'm all set here. Duncan, this is Eleanora Pacelli. You know, Arthur Pacelli's granddaughter? And of course, you know Ann, his wife. Ms. Pacelli, this is Duncan Reeves, an okay ranger at the state park."

"And his best friend," Duncan said, chuckling. "He always forgets that part. It's nice to meet you both."

He nodded to them, hefted his cooler, and carefully boarded the boat. Russell paused to say, "We'll be in touch, Ms. Pacelli," before following him, leaving Ellie with a bundle of nerves in her stomach. She didn't want to be in touch; no, she wanted this whole thing to be over with, and Ben's killer to be caught. She most certainly didn't want to be involved in the case any more than she absolutely had to.

Chapter Eight

"Don't be silly, Ellie. Russell doesn't really think you killed Ben," Shannon said, adjusting her sunglasses.

"I don't know about that. You didn't see him. He looked so... serious," Ellie told her friend. It was the next day, and they were walking down Main Street together, window shopping as they considered what to get for lunch.

"Russ always looks serious. He's a serious guy. I think the last time I saw him crack a smile was at my wedding. But he's good at what he does, and he's not going to think you killed Ben unless you actually did it." She peered at Ellie over her sunglasses, her blue eyes curious. "You didn't, did you?"

"No!" Hands on her hips, she glared at her friend. "Don't be ridiculous. Why would I kill Ben?"

"I don't know. Maybe you don't like roses." Shannon shrugged. "You'd be surprised what petty things people kill each other over."

"Like you'd know," Ellie snorted. "I know you're a reporter, but come on, this is Kittiport. The most brutal crime you've seen before this was what? Some kids vandalizing the library?"

"Yeah, yeah. Kittiport isn't the most exciting town to be a journalist in. I do watch a lot of crime shows, though. If you *did* kill him, tell me now so I can get the scoop."

"I hate to disappoint you—I'm sure a story like that would get you a lot more readers than your columns about quilting contests—but I'm innocent in all of this."

"You're no fun," Shannon said good-naturedly. "On the other hand, if you're innocent, Russ will know. He's a good guy, all right? He doesn't want to waste his time barking up the wrong tree. He doesn't have it out for you or anything, so relax. You'll be fine, Ben's killer will get caught, and we'll all be able to go back to not locking our doors at night."

"Okay," Ellie sighed. "I'll try to put it all out of my mind for now. Tomorrow I've got to go over the new chore schedule and rules with the employees at the pizzeria, and they're not going to like it one bit.

I've got enough on my plate without worrying about Ben's murder, too. I'll leave that to the professionals."

"Good idea. Hey, I know just what you need." Shannon's mischievous grin was back.

"What?"

"A calzone." She nodded at a brightly colored shop across the street with *Cheesaroni Calzones* in bright letters over the door. Next to it was a shop called Elkton Carpentry, with a *Permanently Closed* sign in the door. Ellie felt a pang.

"Wouldn't eating at a calzone place make me a traitor to Papa Pacelli's?" she asked. "Calzones are just a step down from pizza, after all."

"Cheesaroni *is* in direct competition with your place, yeah. But don't think of it as being a traitor… think of it as undercover research. We'll go in, see what makes Cheesaroni Calzones so great, and as an added bonus, we'll walk out with a delicious meal."

"Oh, all right. Now you've got me curious to see if these calzones are actually something special or not."

They turned out to be pretty good. She and Shannon sat down at a table in the corner and dug in. Ellie had decided to go with the artichoke spinach calzone, and didn't regret her choice one bit. The flavors of real ricotta and Parmesan cheese gave the dish a richness that was almost sinful. Cheesaroni didn't skimp on the filling, unlike some other calzone specialty places she had been to, and even after eating the entire thing, she didn't have one complaint.

"I'm glad we stopped here, although I'm starting to regret leaving the cars so far away," Ellie said, leaning back in her chair and gazing around at the restaurant. "I can see why this place is doing so well. The food is great, but it's not just that. Look at how clean everything is, and how friendly the server was. Service makes or breaks a restaurant, I'm telling you."

"So what are you going to do about it?" Shannon asked, poking at the remains of her own calzone. "Do you think you're going to end up firing anyone at the pizzeria?"

"I don't want to," Ellie admitted. "I think that the employees that are there now are mostly good people, they just haven't had the right encouragement. I hope that they'll be willing to work on improving."

"That's optimistic of you. I think—" She broke off as a commotion started near the cash register. The person behind the register, a man in his thirties, was not quite shouting, but was talking loudly at a younger employee. His face was beet red, and his hands were clenched in fists.

"What do you mean you told that family to go to

Papa Pacelli's? That was a big family. You cost us at least thirty bucks! That place is garbage, anyway. They don't deserve the money."

The kid quailed. "I'm sorry, Mr. Dunham, but they said they wanted pizza, and Pacelli's was the only place I could think of…"

"If someone walks in here wanting pizza, you don't tell them to go to a pizza place! You tell them that calzone is just like a pizza, just easier to eat, and then you sell them two."

The man the younger employee had called Mr. Dunham gave a sharp huff of anger and stomped through the doors that led to the kitchen. The kid, who looked like he was on the verge of tears, made his way over to Ellie and Shannon's table to clear their trash.

"Who was that?" Ellie asked. "Is he your boss?"

The young employee nodded. "Yeah. That's Jeffrey Dunham. He owns this place."

"He shouldn't have treated you that way." She reached into her purse and took out enough cash for a sizable tip, which she stuffed into the kid's hand. "Here, take this. You deserve it. No one should have to deal with a boss like that."

Shannon gave her a sideways look once they hit the sidewalk. "What was that about?"

"I felt bad for him," Ellie told her friend. "And, well, a bit guilty. If Jeffrey Dunham is that worried about a little competition, then he's going to be even more upset once he sees just how well Papa Pacelli's does under good management. On the other hand, if he's the sort of person the pizzeria has to compete against, then I'm not too worried."

"Well look at you," the other woman said. "I'd know that determined look anywhere. If I was a betting woman, I'd put down money that you'll run him out of business within the year."

"Nothing can stop a Pacelli once we've set our mind to something," Ellie said. "And there's no way I'm going to let a jerk like that badmouth my family's restaurant."

Chapter Nine

When Ellie sat down that evening for a New England-style dinner with her grandmother—complete with a scrumptious seafood chowder—her mind was still on her plan for getting the pizzeria's good name back. It would take a lot of hard work and dedication, but she was prepared for it.

"You haven't told me about the encounter with Sheriff Ward from yesterday yet," her grandmother said while they ate. "He seemed *very* interested in you."

"Nonna," Ellie said, almost choking on a bite of chowder. "He was interested in me because I'm a *suspect*. I was the last one to see Ben alive, after all. And the first one to see him dead. Why did you chime in about the gun, anyway? What do you even need a gun for?"

"Personal protection, my dear. This is a nice house, and there were a few break-ins nearby a while back. Your grandfather thought it was a good idea. I keep it in my nightstand drawer."

Ellie shook her head, not quite sure how she felt about her octogenarian grandmother packing heat.

"You know, the sheriff is a very nice man once you get to know him," Ann continued. "I voted for him last election. Or maybe I voted for the other guy… well, either way, he's a good sheriff. You could do worse."

"Let's at least wait until the guy doesn't think I'm a murderer before you start trying to pair me up with him, okay, Nonna? Now let's eat… I want to get back to Papa's study and go over his files again. I feel like I'm missing something."

After cleaning up after dinner, Ellie shut herself in the study while her grandmother went to bed. The stack of records waiting for her was nothing new— she had already gone once through the entire pile, which documented nearly every month of the pizzeria's financial history since it opened. Still, there was something that kept drawing her back to the pile. She kept telling herself she would go to bed after going through the next folder, and then the next, and gradually the night wore on, inching toward morning with her still sitting at her grandfather's desk.

Ellie jerked awake, blinking groggily and looking down at the desk where she had been resting her head. The papers were a mess, she still wasn't any closer to finding the clue to the pizzeria's financial hardships that she had been looking for, and it was nearing three in the morning. Falling asleep at the desk had left her with a kink in her neck, which she rubbed gingerly before beginning the task of stacking the papers into semi-neat piles.

Suddenly she froze, a file clutched in her hand as her heart rate jumped up a notch. She might still be half asleep, but she could have sworn that she had just heard a voice. She listened hard, but the old house was silent. She was just about to relax and brush it off as a figment of an overactive imagination when she heard it again.

Quietly, from beyond the heavy oak door of her grandfather's study, sounded a quiet "Hello?"

It was a woman's voice; of that she was sure. Ellie felt a chill seep into her bones. She didn't believe in ghosts, and she had to keep telling herself that as she eased out of the chair and made her way silently toward the door. A quick glance down at Bunny, who had been napping by her feet a moment before, showed her that she wasn't going insane—the dog heard it too.

It's probably Nonna, she told herself. *Either she's sleepwalking, or she's just confused. She is old, after all, and I think she mentioned that she has had trouble sleeping since grandfather died.*

"Hello? Hi. How are you?"

The voice was clearer now that she was standing near the study door, and it did sound almost like her grandmother's voice. It was off just enough to give her goosebumps. Something wasn't right.

Telling herself not to be such a wimp, Ellie eased the study door open and slipped out into the hallway, the files still clutched in her hand. She heard the voice again, much more clearly this time.

"Hi. Good birdie. How are you?"

Feeling like an idiot, Ellie realized what the voice was right before she rounded the corner to see Marlowe's cage next to the stairs. Not planning to stay up as late as she had, she had left the light on in the entrance way, and had evidently kept the bird up. She had never heard the parrot talk before, and was surprised by just how human her voice sounded.

"Hi. You almost gave me a heart attack," she said. The bird turned her head to one side, staring at her with one eye. "Are you going to say anything else, or do you only talk when no one's around?"

Marlowe remained silent.

"Well, sorry for keeping you up. I'm sure you're just as tired as I am. Let me just return these papers to the—"

She broke off, staring at the papers in her hand. It was all so obvious, all of a sudden. She rushed back to the study and spread the files out in front of her, squinting as she tried to read the dates on her grandfather's handwritten notes. There it was, plain as day. Why hadn't she seen it before?

The pizzeria had been doing well up until about two years ago. The restaurant's profits first started to drop the month after her grandfather had hired Xavier as the manager, and they had been dropping slowly but steadily ever since. She still needed more proof, but Ellie was all but certain that the pizzeria's manager had *something* to do with the restaurant's financial trouble. The only question that remained was whether it was due to his poor management skills, or something much more sinister.

Chapter Ten

Ellie hurried into the pizzeria early the next morning, hoping to have a few good hours to look for the proof that she needed before the employees started showing up. All of her grandfather's files were based on the sales records that Xavier had given him. To prove her theory right, she needed the original records, which meant trying to figure out the ancient lump of a machine that they used as a cash register. It was easier than she had expected—the instruction manual was easily found online. After she printed out the old receipts, she spent a couple of hours comparing them to the records Xavier had given her grandfather. She found what she was looking for easily enough, and could hardly believe her eyes.

By the time Xavier showed up to unlock the doors

and fire up the ovens, she was shaking with rage. She waited as he and Jacob performed the morning rituals to get the pizzeria ready for the day. When they finished at last, she called Xavier into the dining area and slammed the pile of receipts and her grandfather's reports down on a table in front of him.

"Explain this," she hissed.

"I don't know what you're talking about," Xavier said, but he had gone pale. Jacob was watching curiously from the register as he counted the drawer.

"Every single month you gave my grandfather the records of the pizzeria's sales," she said, her tone dangerous. "And every single month, the total on the records you gave him was significantly lower thanwhat the receipts tallied up to. Sometimes by more than a thousand dollars. My grandfather trusted you to run this restaurant, and you repaid him by lying to him and stealing from him."

Xavier's eyes darted down to the printed receipts, then back up to Ellie's face. She could see the gears in his head turning as he tried to work up an excuse. She wasn't having any of it.

"You're fired. Get out. I don't want to see you around here again."

Without saying a word, Xavier stomped away. He passed through the kitchen doors, and she heard a *bang* as he kicked something on his way out. Still fuming, she turned to Jacob.

"Did you know about any of this?" she asked him.

He shook his head quickly. "Xavier didn't let anyone else tally the monthly totals."

She stared at him for a moment, trying to gauge whether or not she believed him. At last she nodded and began gathering her evidence up.

"We'll have to figure out what to do to replace him but I'm sure we can manage for now. Without him siphoning money away from the restaurant, this place should start doing much better."

With Xavier gone for good, Ellie decided to begin taking over his duties where she could right away. She had always enjoyed cooking, and making the pizzas came easily to her. What she found a bit more difficult was the task of juggling her duties in the kitchen with her duties to the customers. The first time Jacob left her alone in the pizzeria that afternoon to go deliver a pizza, she accidentally burned one of the orders after getting distracted by a conversation with a customer. After that, she forced herself to keep a closer eye on the clock. She couldn't very well expect her employees to stay focused at work if she couldn't manage it herself.

She was just beginning to get used to the rhythm

of the fast-paced work when Russell Ward walked into the restaurant, completely interrupting her tempo. She knew as soon as she laid eyes on his face that he wasn't there for a pizza.

"What happened?" she asked when he reached the register, feeling a spark of fear at the sight of his grim expression.

"There was an intruder at your grandmother's house," he said, lowering his voice in an effort to keep their conversation private from the couple at the corner booth a few feet away. "She's all right, but I think you should come with me."

Ellie's heart began to pound. Someone had tried to break in to her grandmother's house? She wondered if anything else could go wrong. First, Ben's murder, then finding out that Xavier had been stealing from the pizzeria for years, and now this. Maybe returning to Kittiport hadn't been such a good idea after all.

"I can't just leave," she told the sheriff, glancing over at the couple in the corner booth. "Jacob's out on a delivery, and I just fired my manager. I'm the only one here. Is she hurt? Is she scared?"

"She's fine," he assured her. "She's actually a lot more composed than most people half her age would be. When should your delivery guy be back?"

"Umm…" she glanced at the clock. "Any minute,

hopefully." *If he doesn't pull what he did last week, and stay out for another two hours.*

"I'll wait," the sheriff said. "Something seriously odd is going on here, and I want to get to the bottom of it as quickly as possible. Your grandfather was a good man, and helped me out a couple of times; I'd like to return the favor by catching whoever broke into his house as quickly as possible."

Chapter Eleven

When Jacob returned from his delivery, Ellie gave him a quick rundown of what had happened, and left him in charge of the pizzeria with instructions not to accept any more deliveries for the rest of the day. The young man looked momentarily panicked at the thought of being left in charge of the pizzeria himself, but assured her that he was up to the task. As soon as she caught her employee up to speed, Ellie left with the sheriff, and followed him back home in her own car.

There were two cruisers pulled into the driveway at her grandmother's house. Ellie parked on the grass next to one of them, and hurried inside, Russell hot on her heels. She found her grandmother in the living room with Bunny on her lap, and the two deputies sitting on chairs and drinking tea.

"What are you doing here?" Russell asked gruffly. Ellie looked around in surprise to see that he was talking to his friend, the one who worked as a ranger in the state park. He was wearing a dark green jacket and looked harried.

"I was passing by and saw Bethany's cruiser. Thought I'd see if I could be of any help," he explained. "I was heading toward here anyway after I heard the gunshot. We've been having trouble with poachers lately."

Russell nodded. "I take it Bethany told you what happened?"

"No one's told *me* what happened," Ellie cut in. She sat down on the couch next to her grandmother, touching the older woman gently on the arm. "Are you okay, Nonna?"

"I'm fine, dear. Would you like some tea?"

Ellie looked at the teapot on the coffee table and shook her head. "Will someone please just tell me what happened?"

Russell nodded to Bethany, and the young deputy began telling the story.

"About two hours ago, we got a call down at the station reporting a gunshot in the area. I was dispatched to go investigate, and when I arrived on the scene, I found your grandmother standing outside the house near the back door holding a firearm. I requested that she put the weapon down, which she did, at which time I secured the firearm. When questioned, Mrs. Pacelli told me that she had been napping when she heard the sound of breaking glass. Fearing for her life, she removed her gun from her nightstand drawer and went to investigate. She found a masked intruder in her kitchen, who she claims was holding a gun in his hand. She fired a round, but is unsure whether she hit him. The intruder fled." Bethany hesitated, glancing up at Russell. He gave her an encouraging nod.

"You're doing well," he said. "You did everything by the book. Go on."

Ellie remembered what the woman had told her, about being new to the job. *Well, she's certainly had quite the exciting start to her career,* she thought.

"I called for backup, and was told you would be here shortly, Sheriff. Then I did a cursory search of the premises and immediate property to ensure the intruder wasn't hiding somewhere. I didn't find him, but I did find this. The intruder must have dropped it after Ann... Mrs. Pacelli shot at him." The female deputy picked up a plastic bag from the coffee table.

Inside was a second plastic bag, and a black handgun. Ellie shivered.

"Wait… why is it double bagged?" she asked, leaning forward to peer at it more closely. She glanced up at the sheriff, who looked impressed.

"The outer bag is an evidence bag," he explained. "The inner bag looks like some sort of bread bag, and the gun was in it when Bethany here found it."

"I don't understand," Ellie said, confused. "Why would the intruder have his gun in a plastic bag? He couldn't use it like that."

Russell nodded. "I wondered the same thing. It will take some testing to prove, of course, but I have a theory."

"What is it?" she asked when he hesitated.

"It's just a theory, mind you," he said. "But this is a 9mm pistol, the same caliber that killed Ben. Someone broke into your house with that gun encased in a bag—likely to keep it from getting their finger-prints on it or picking up any fibers. Like I said, it's just a guess… but I'm thinking that whoever broke in wasn't planning on taking anything. They wanted to leave something."

Ellie cocked her head. "Are you saying… someone broke in to plant the gun?"

"I'm saying it's a possibility," Russ said seriously.

"We'll send the gun off to forensics to get tested. They should be able to determine whether it shot the bullet that killed Ben. If it's a match, we'll be that much closer to catching his killer—and I'll owe you a real apology for ever suspecting you."

After the sheriff and his deputies left, Ellie helped her grandmother clean up the impromptu tea party. She was surprised by how well the elderly woman seemed to be holding up. If *she* had been forced to shoot at an armed intruder, she was certain she would be much more shaken. Her grandmother was a tough woman for sure.

They chatted while they cleaned, going over the break-in, and then delving into the fiasco with Xavier. Her grandmother seemed more upset by that, and Ellie felt a fresh rush of anger toward the young man. How dare he steal from her family's restaurant? She wasn't sure what her next step should be—she didn't want him to get off without consequences but she also wasn't sure she was prepared to go to court over the issue. It was something that she wanted to talk to her grandmother about, but later.

"Do you think what the sheriff said is right?" she asked. "About the intruder coming here to plant the gun and make it look like I killed Ben? Why would anyone want to do that? I haven't been here long enough to make any enemies."

"I don't know, Ellie," her grandmother said. "But either way, I don't think either of us will be getting good sleep for a long time."

Chapter Twelve

Ellie was reluctant to leave her grandmother alone at the house after the break-in, but she didn't really have a choice. After she convinced her nonna to install motion detectors and a floodlight by the back door she felt a bit better, but she was still relieved when she came back to find the house secure and its occupants safe. For the first time, she wished that the little papillon was more prone to barking. The little dog was used to living in a city apartment, however, and wouldn't be at all perturbed by strangers' footsteps.

As the days passed and nothing else out of the ordinary happened, Ellie gradually began to relax. Business at the pizzeria was picking up now that the restaurant was kept clean, and she stayed on top of the employees about providing good customer service.

She had discovered that she had a real talent for making pizzas, and by the time her second week was up, she rarely had to consult the recipe book when putting together orders.

When her friend Shannon suggested a boating trip that weekend with some other ladies that she knew, Ellie was more than happy to accept. She had been working hard, and figured she deserved a break; plus, it would give her a chance to meet some new people and maybe expand her social circle a bit. In a town as small as Kittiport, where everyone already knew everyone else, it could be hard to make new friends, so she jumped on the opportunity of an afternoon boating with the girls.

"This is the life," Ellie sighed, popping open an ice-cold can of diet soda from the cooler. She was sitting in the shaded cabin of the *Eleanora* with Shannon and two other women whom she had met less than an hour ago. Shannon was navigating the boat out of the marina toward a spot that she claimed had a wonderful view of some dramatic cliffs over-looking the Atlantic.

"Thanks for suggesting that we use your boat," said the older of the two other women. "It's great to meet you at last. Shannon's told us both so much about you." Liz was a hard-working single mother of two girls, both of whom were now off at college. Ellie had taken an instant liking to her, and shot her a bright smile.

"It's my pleasure," she said earnestly. "I'm glad for the chance to kick back and relax. It's been a crazy two weeks."

"Sorry again about James deciding to go on a fishing trip with his buddies at the last minute. I completely forgot to tell him I was planning on using the boat today. You really saved the day, Ellie," Shannon said. "It would have been a shame to cancel our plans. It's a gorgeous day."

It really was. The blue sky had only a few puffy white clouds in it, and the sun glittered off the waves. With a steady but gentle breeze, the weather was perfect for sun bathing without getting too hot. The trip to Shannon's favorite spot didn't take long, and within half an hour they were anchored a few hundred yards offshore, with stark jagged cliffs topped by windswept white pines standing guard above them. The ocean was dotted with sailboats, visible from a distance thanks to their brilliantly white sails, and the silence was interrupted only occasionally by the growl of a motorboat speeding through the waves.

The women lay in the sun on towels on the deck of the boat and chatted. Ellie, being the newcomer, mostly listened at first, joining in occasionally with stories about her own life. She didn't have any kids, but she could commiserate about terrible bosses and even worse boyfriends with the best of them. She was just beginning to feel accepted by Liz and the other woman, Margaret, when the talk turned to Ben.

His death wasn't something that she particularly wanted to discuss, but she couldn't find a good way to get out of answering their questions. Even Shannon seemed morbidly interested in what had happened.

"Poor guy," her friend said after Ellie retold the story of finding him behind the pizzeria. "Do you ever wonder if he'd still be alive if you hadn't gone on that date with him?"

Of course she did. She had lain awake at night for hours wondering what would have happened if she and Ben had gone on their date another night. Had his murder been the random work of a mugger? If so, then his death might have been nothing more than a cruel coincidence. On the other hand, if Ben's killer had targeted him specifically, then he likely would have been killed either way. She didn't know which was worse—to think that his death might have been nothing more than a twist of fate, or to think that Ben had somehow managed to make an enemy dangerous enough to have killed him.

She was saved from answering Shannon's question by the sound of a boat's engine drawing near. All four women sat up, their eyes on the fishing boat that was speeding toward them from the open ocean. Ellie felt the stirrings of unease in her stomach. With a killer on the loose, had it been smart for the four of them to come out here alone?

Her concerns were quickly put to rest by the bright smile that appeared on Shannon's face.

"It's just James and the guys," she said. "He knows I love this spot. I bet he thought he'd surprise us with a visit."

To Ellie's surprise, she recognized all of the faces on the boat that pulled up alongside them. There was James, of course, who looked like a younger and less serious version of his brother Russell. Standing next to him was the park ranger, Duncan, who nodded at her curtly, and Jeffrey Dunham, the man who owned Cheesaroni Calzones. He didn't seem to recognize her, for which she was grateful. She remembered how angry he had gotten at just the mention of Papa Pacelli's, and wasn't sure she wanted him to know that it was her family's restaurant. From what she had seen that day that she and Shannon had gotten calzones, Dunham had some serious anger issues.

"Any luck?" Shannon said to her husband. He shook his head.

"They're just not biting today. We're going to head in, but I wanted to stop and see how you ladies were doing first."

"We're enjoying ourselves. Ellie's grandmother's boat is nice, isn't it? It's the perfect size for the four of us." She hesitated, then added, "We were just talking about Ben Elkton. Have you heard anything new from Russ about him?"

"No," James said. "Do you know anything, Duncan?"

Duncan shrugged. He was wearing a long-sleeved jacket, and seemed uncomfortable in the hot weather. He gave Ellie a long look that she wasn't sure what to make of before speaking. "Russell doesn't have any new suspects that I know of, no."

Jeffrey Dunham suddenly spoke up. "Hey, you're that Pacelli woman, aren't you?" He was staring right at her, and his expression was far from friendly. "You're the one that's trying to fix up that pizza place."

"I am," she said reluctantly. "Eleanora Pacelli. It's nice to meet you."

He grunted and turned to James. "C'mon, let's get outta here, man."

James sighed, but said a quick goodbye to his wife and started up the boat's onboard engine again. He gave a nod of farewell to the other women, then eased the vessel away from the *Eleanora*.

"Have a nice time!" he called over the growl of the engine.

Ellie watched the boat slowly draw away, then turned to her friend with a puzzled expression on her face.

"What was that all about?" she asked. "Why do I get the feeling that both Duncan and Jeffrey already hate me?"

"They're all part of the group that Ben played poker with," Shannon explained gently. "From what James has said, some of the guys think Ben would still be alive if it wasn't for you, since he got killed while bringing you flowers. I'm sure it will all blow over soon enough, so I wouldn't worry about it too much. Duncan, at least, should come around. Jeffrey's just a jerk, so I wouldn't expect too much out of him. Don't let them get you down."

Her friend smiled at her encouragingly, then straightened her towel out and lay back down. Ellie settled down too, more reluctantly. Her mind was buzzing. She felt like something important was hovering just beyond the reach of her memory, some-

Chapter Thirteen

Ellie was in a sour mood when she returned to work on Monday. Her encounter with the men on the boat had stayed with her for the rest of the weekend. She kept turning it over in her mind, feeling like she was missing *something*, but unsure as to exactly what. *Maybe I just can't stand the fact that those two guys seem to hate me,* she thought as she unlocked the pizzeria's back door. *I didn't* do *anything, and it's just unfair. I didn't ask for any of this to happen.*

She shoved open the door and walked inside the building, only to be assaulted by a vile stench. Gagging, she slapped at the light switch. What she found made her stagger backwards in shock.

Every inch of the kitchen had been splattered in pizza dough. The fridge was hanging open, the food in it spoiled. The heat had been cranked up, probably to accelerate the process. There was no way that any of this could be an accident. No, this could only be one thing; sabotage. And Ellie had a feeling that she knew just who did it.

Digging through her purse, she pulled out the card that Sheriff Ward had given her the day she had discovered Ben's body. She punched his number into her phone, ignoring the little voice inside her that warned that a wrecked kitchen wasn't exactly a crime worthy of a sheriff's attention. She didn't care—she wanted only one thing; to see Xavier handcuffed and carted away like the thieving vandal he was.

"Are you sure you locked the door?" Russell asked. He was standing just outside the pizzeria's back entrance with her, his hands on his hips as he stared at the stinky mess inside.

"Yes, I'm sure," Ellie said. "I spent the last twenty-five years of my life in Chicago; I *always* lock my doors. I was the last one out of here on Friday. And besides, the door was locked when I got here."

"How many people besides you have a key?"

She paused, counting people off in her head. "Well, my grandmother does. Rose, Clara, and Jacob all do. And, darn it! Xavier still does—I was so upset when I fired him that I forgot to ask for his key back.

I don't think anyone else has a key, but I can't be sure."

"I'm going to go out on a limb here and say your grandmother didn't do it," he said. She thought she saw his lips twitch. Did he find this *funny?* "That leaves us with four suspects."

"No, it leaves us with one suspect," she snapped. "It was Xavier. I know it was."

He turned toward her and said, with infuriating calmness, "Do you have any proof of that, Ms. Pacelli?"

"Not exactly. But I shouldn't need any. He's the obvious one."

"Well, I'll go talk to him for you. Whether he confesses or not, I suggest changing the locks on this place and issuing new keys to those that need them. There's a locksmith just down the road from you."

"That will be the first thing I do after I get this mess cleaned up," she said. "I can't believe this. Can nothing go right for once?"

"If it will cheer you up, I've got some good news for you," the sheriff said.

"You found Ben's killer?" she asked hopefully.

"Not quite. But we did get the forensics back on the gun that the intruder dropped in your yard. It's a match. It's the gun that shot the bullet that killed Ben Elkton."

"Oh." She blinked. "So that means... I'm not a suspect anymore?"

"Not unless you can be two places at once." He smiled at her. "This brings us one step closer to catching the guy that did it. Now, you get to work on cleaning up this mess, and I'll go see if I can track down this disgruntled ex-employee of yours."

Scraping the spoiled dough out of the kitchen was not fun, but after Rose arrived and began helping, the job went faster. Once the kitchen was clean, they were faced with another problem: replacing the spoiled vegetables, meats, and cheese that had been in the fridge. They normally only got deliveries once a week, and wouldn't have another one for four days. Ellie ended up handing Rose her credit card, an extensive list, and instructions to buy everything she could find at the local grocery store.

"Just get what you can and hurry back," she told the young woman. "I'll start making more dough. We're going to open late today, but we *are* going to open."

A few minutes after Rose left, Ellie was surprised by a knock on the pizzeria's back door. She opened it with flour-covered hands to find the sheriff standing outside.

"I found Xavier," he said. "It's an interesting story, and you're not going to like it."

She invited him in. "I've got to get this batch of dough done or we won't have anything to make pizzas with," she told him. "But please, I want to hear this."

"Well, it turns out that your employee now works for Jeffrey Dunham. I take it you know what business he owns?"

"Cheesaroni Calzones," she said with a sigh. "I'm familiar with him."

"My brother's his friend, but I can't say I like him myself. My opinion of him is even lower now, in fact." The sheriff sighed. "Jeffrey's acting as Xavier's alibi, and swears the kid didn't go anywhere near this place at all yesterday. Xavier was next to him the whole time, snickering. I've got the feeling that the pair of them were behind this, but with no evidence, I can't do anything. I'm sorry."

"Great," she said with a groan. "The two men that hate me the most right now are working together. Can this week get any worse?"

"It can always get worse," the sheriff pointed out.

"But I'll keep an eye on them for you. And get those locks changed as soon as possible."

He turned to leave, but hesitated on the threshold. "I mean it, Ellie. I don't know what we're dealing with here. Be careful."

Chapter Fourteen

"All right, you guys. I have an idea."

It was the Thursday after the attempted sabotage of the pizzeria, and Ellie had been brainstorming ways to bounce back ever since. She thought that she finally had it. Jacob, Rose, and Clara were all sitting at the small table in the kitchen, staring at her with expressions ranging from cautious to mildly interested as they waited for her to tell them her grand plan.

"We're going to host a grand re-opening next Saturday," she told them. "The pizzeria will be closed to the public that Friday, but I expect all three of you to be here. We're going to scrub this place from top to bottom again, and I'll also be going over some new guidelines for the employees at the same time. When we re-open, we're going to be a completely new restaurant, understood? No more sub-par service. No more delivery of cold pizzas. No more sticky booths and greasy plates. I know it's going to take some effort and change on your part, but I hope you'll stick with me through it. Any questions?"

Jacob raised his hand tentatively. "Erm, when are we getting a new manager?"

"You already have one." Ellie beamed at him. "Me."

"Why would you want to do that?" he asked. "Didn't you have some fancy job in Chicago? Why would you want to manage a pizza joint after that?"

"I did," she said. "But I've discovered something in the past couple of weeks. I like working here. I enjoy being involved with the day-to-day running of the place. I know it's just a pizza joint, but it's more than that to me… it's my family's legacy. And I want to be involved with it."

"Cool, I guess," he said with a shrug, turning his attention back to his cellphone.

"One more thing," Ellie said. She waited until all eyes were on her before speaking again. "I'm going to institute a friendly competition. Each week, one of you will design a pizza of the week, which we'll feature on the menu. At the end of the month, the person whose pizza did the best will get a prize. Nothing big, but I think it will be a great way to get everyone involved more. What do you think?"

She was pleased to see her employees' eyes light up. The thought of competing against each other seemed to spark something in them that the daily drudge of working behind the counter had tamped down. She knew that working at a pizzeria wasn't exactly a dream job for any of them, but there was no reason they couldn't still enjoy it. A friendly competition would be a good way to bring them out of their shells and get them interacting with each other more —not to mention, it would keep the pizzeria's menu fresh for the customers. She had a couple of other ideas to help make their menu more interesting as well, but those would have to wait for another day. *Baby steps*, she told herself. *I've got to get this place's reputation turned around before anything else, and I don't want to bite off more than I can chew.*

They began spreading flyers around Kittiport the next day. One benefit of having such young employees was that they were more than happy to spend their work day walking around town with a stapler and a stack of flyers. Before long, every telephone pole had at least one flyer on it advertising the grand re-opening of Papa Pacelli's a week from Saturday. Shannon even offered to write a blurb about the pizzeria in her column in the *Kittiport Daily News*, the town's local paper.

One thing that Ellie hadn't been expecting was how many new customers they got even before the big day. People who hadn't been to the pizzeria in years stopped in, amazed at the change in the restaurant. More than one person complimented her on how much better the place looked, which made her positively glow with pride. She hadn't felt this connected with her work in years, and especially not when she was working at the big financial firm back in Chicago. For the first time, she was almost glad that she had found out about Kenneth's affair. She was happier now than she had ever been when she was engaged to him, and the realization that maybe she didn't need a man in her life to feel fulfilled was freeing.

Chapter Fifteen

The day of the grand re-opening dawned cold and chilly.

"Perfect pizza weather," her grandmother said as she buttoned up her jacket.

"I suppose..." Ellie peered up at the overcast sky. "I hope it doesn't rain. What if no one shows up?"

"Don't worry so much, dear. You've done a wonderful job these past few weeks. I'm sure the pizzeria will be bustling today."

"I sure hope you're right, Nonna." She took her grandmother's arm and helped the frail old lady down the front porch's stairs. "If this doesn't work out, I don't know what else to try."

The two of them arrived at the pizzeria before anyone else. Ellie got her grandmother settled in a chair at one of the window tables, then walked slowly through the dining room. She, Jacob, Rose, and Clara had spent hours yesterday cleaning and decorating. Red and black helium balloons were tied to the chair backs in alternating pairs, matching the tilework on the walls. A big banner reading *Grand Re-opening!* was hanging over the register, and a fresh stack of paper menus was sitting on the counter. They had held a drawing to determine which of the employees would get to go first in designing a pizza of the week, and Clara had won. A photo of her chicken pesto pizza was on the front of the menu; just looking at it made Ellie's mouth water.

Not much had changed in the kitchen, but she walked through it anyway. The new lock on the employee entrance gleamed, and she felt reassured to see it. All week she had been worrying about Xavier and Jeffrey trying to do something to wreck the pizzeria's big day, but so far she'd seen neither hide nor hair of them. Surely they wouldn't try anything once the place was teeming with customers… would they?

Ellie bit back her anxiety. To distract herself, she pulled open the fridge and double-checked all of the pizza dough. They had the original dough, used to make thin-crust round pizzas, in addition to thick-crust and deep-dish doughs. She had been surprised to learn that the different sorts of crusts were actually made out of different types of dough, each one requiring different methods to shape and cook it. Making good pizza was an art, and at times she still felt very much the novice.

By the time Jacob, Rose, and Clara arrived, Ellie's anxiety was back in full swing. She kept glancing at the clock as they set up for the day. Half an hour until the doors opened… twenty minutes… ten minutes…

Suddenly, almost before she knew it, it was time to go unlock the front doors and welcome the town of Kittiport in.

The turnout was better than she had hoped. Customers wandered in and out, some buying pizzas to go, others choosing to eat in for the first time. Jacob was kept busy rushing back and forth to deliver pizzas and pick up orders. Ellie couldn't have been happier. Her plan had worked—the entire town knew that Papa Pacelli's was back and better than ever.

Even more rewarding than the crowded restaurant was the sight of the smile on her grandmother's face. Were those tears in her eyes? "You really did it, Ellie. You brought your grandfather's dream back to life."

"This is just the beginning," Ellie told her, leaning down to give the old woman a hug. "I should be the one thanking you. I—"

She broke off, her gaze fixed on an all-too-familiar form in the crowd.

"Hold on, Nonna, I'll be right back," she promised her grandmother, forcing a smile back on her face before she noticed that anything was wrong.

She edged her way through the crowd, keeping her eye on Xavier all the while. She wasn't surprised to see his new boss, Jeffrey Dunham, not far away. It wasn't until she saw Xavier pause by the counter to talk to Rose that she stopped. She was just close enough to hear their conversation—barely—and didn't want to risk having either of the men see her.

"This place doesn't look half bad," Xavier said. Ellie saw his eyes take in the banner and balloons. "Art's granddaughter really tried to go all out, huh? Guess she thought it would make up for not seeing him all those years. I should tell that cow just how often he talked about her. Though I doubt she'd care —she's pretty cold-hearted, isn't she?"

Ellie bristled.

"You shouldn't call her that, Xavier," Rose said sounding disapproving. "Ms. Pacelli's actually really nice."

"Yeah, right," Xavier snorted. "Please tell me you don't actually like working for her. Look what she did to me. She *fired* me, for no reason at all."

"You *were* stealing from the restaurant," Rose said, beginning to sound annoyed. "That's a pretty good reason. It's your own fault."

"Yeah, well, whatever. This place won't be successful for long, and you'll be sorry you didn't quit and join me at Cheesaroni."

"What's your problem, Xav?" the young woman snapped. "If you don't like it here, why'd you come back?"

"Jeffrey says it's best to know our competition," Xavier said, tapping his nose with one finger. "He wanted to swing by to see if this place had actually managed to attract any attention."

"Well, as you can see, we're doing really well," Rose said, her tone haughty. "Probably better than that Cheesaroni place. Why'd you decide to work there, anyway?"

"I wanted a chance to get back at Ms. P," he said, shrugging. "It's a lot better than working here, that's for sure. I don't have anyone looking over my shoulder anymore, and the boss is cool. He even let me go to a poker game with him last weekend, and I won a bunch of money."

Something jogged Ellie's memory. She frowned, trying to figure out what it was. Meanwhile, Xavier was still talking.

"Oh, and he just put in a bid for that carpentry place next door to Cheesaroni. That Ben dude owned it, and Jeffrey's been trying to get it forever. He really wants to expand."

Ellie felt her eyes go wide. She remembered seeing Ben's abandoned shop next to the calzone place, but she hadn't thought much of it then. Now, however, it took on a whole new meaning.

I know who killed Ben Elkton, she thought. *And he's in my restaurant right now.*

Chapter Sixteen

She swept her gaze over the crowd, finally finding Jeffrey Dunham near the soda fridge. He had an annoyed look on his face, and kept fiddling with his cellphone. Without pausing to think, Ellie pushed her way through the crowd toward him, finally emerging near his right elbow. He looked down at her coldly.

"What do you want?" he asked. "Your flyers did say *everyone* was invited."

"I know you killed Ben," she hissed, glaring at him with her hands on her hips. She was between him and the exit, and had every intention of blocking him if he tried to make a run for it.

"What the heck are you talking about, lady?" he asked. "Ben was my friend."

"I know you're trying to buy his carpentry store so that you can expand your calzone business."

"So? That doesn't mean I killed him." He blinked, then lowered his voice. "Wait. Does this mean you *didn't* kill him?"

"Why would I kill Ben?" Her voice squeaked in indignation. "Don't try to turn this around on me."

"Why would *I* kill Ben? We've been friends for over ten years. He'd been talking about selling his store for the last three years running. Kept saying he wanted to get out of town, see the world. I'm the one that convinced him to stick around a while longer. Why would I do that, and then kill him?"

Ellie frowned. "I—" Something wiggled loose in her memory. "The money," she said.

Jeffrey stared at her blankly.

"The poker money," she clarified. Still nothing, no flash of recognition on his face. "The money you owed him. That's why you killed him. You didn't want to pay up."

"Lady, I've got no idea what you're talking about. I've had about enough of this—"

"When we were on our date, he told me that he had won a bunch of money from one of the guys that he played poker with, and was supposed to pick it up that Saturday. You decided you didn't want to pay him, so you tracked him down and shot him outside the pizzeria. Two birds with one stone—you got to keep the money you owed him, and his body being found behind the pizzeria made this place look bad."

"And how on earth would I have known that poor, love-struck Ben was going to leave you a flower in the middle of the night?" Jeffrey snorted.

That stumped Ellie. As she struggled for a retort, another familiar face appeared out of the crowd: Duncan.

"What's going on here?" he asked.

"This woman's losing her mind," Jeffrey said, shaking his head. "She thinks I killed Ben. She's figured out all sorts of reasons, too. I don't need this. I'm done here."

He brushed past her, pausing to add, "Besides, you've got it wrong, sweetheart. I'm not the one that owed Ben money. That'd be Duncan."

With that, he was gone, leaving her alone in the corner with Russell's friend. He stared at her for a long moment, his eyes cold, before turning away.

Ellie stood frozen where she was as she watched him disappear into the crowd. She had been wrong. Oh, she had been so, so wrong. There was one thing that she had been right about, though. Ben *had* been killed because of the money, but it wasn't Jeffrey that killed him... it was Duncan.

When she was able to force herself to move again, she headed straight for the pizzeria's landline in the kitchen. Confronting Jeffrey in the heat of the moment in a crowd was one thing, but she was terrified of Duncan. She had to report what she knew to someone who would know what to do.

The number to the Kittiport sheriff's office was posted next to the phone, along with the fire department and coast guard numbers. Ellie began punching in the digits, but paused partway through when something occurred to her. She was about to accuse a fellow law enforcement officer of murder with no proof. Who would believe her? Best case scenario, they would laugh her off the line. Worst case scenario, Duncan would hear about it and come after her to shut her up.

"So what do I do?" she whispered, feeling miles away from the happy customers on the other side of the door. "Who can I trust?"

Russell immediately came to mind. She didn't know if he would believe her, but she had the feeling he would at least consider what she had to say. All she had to do was call the sheriff's office and ask to speak to him directly. She punched in the rest of the numbers and waited for the other line to ring.

"I'm sorry, he's not in the office right now. Can I take a message?" asked a chipper-voiced secretary when she finally got through.

"No," Ellie said dully. "Thanks."

She set the phone back in the cradle and wracked her brain. The answer, when she found it, was so obvious that she was surprised that she hadn't thought of it sooner. She had his business card, with his cell number on the back. The only problem was; it was out in her car along with her cellphone.

"I'll be right back," Ellie told Clara, who was busy shuffling pizzas between ovens. Her employee gave her a distracted nod.

She slipped out the back door and hurried across the parking lot—which was unusually crowded, thanks to the nearly overwhelming number of customers they were getting—and found her car. Fumbling with her keys, she unlocked it and sat in the driver's seat with the door open, trying to find the sheriff's business card in her messy purse.

"Dang it, I really need to clean this thing out," she muttered.

"I'd say."

Ellie jumped, knocking the purse off the seat. She

turned to see none other than Duncan standing just outside her open driver's door, leaning casually against the neighboring car.

"I thought you might try something like this," he said with a sigh. "Nosy people never know when to stop."

"I... I don't know what you're talking about," she said. "I'm just looking for my lipstick."

"Don't try to pull that with me." He leaned forward, putting a hand on the open car door. Ellie shrank back inside the vehicle.

"Scared?" He chuckled. "Finally. Your instincts are kicking in at last. It would have been better for both of us if they hadn't kicked in at all. You *really* shouldn't go sticking your nose into official police business."

He was toying with her, Ellie realized. The thought gave her a burst of much needed anger that cut through the fear and let her think again.

"I'll stick my nose wherever I want, *especially* when my friends are involved," she said, forcing herself to sit up straighter and hating the tremor in her voice. She met his eyes. "Tell me... just how much did you owe him?"

Duncan looked annoyed, but to her surprise answered. "Ten grand. I have a gambling problem, I know. But I don't have that sort of money, not even close."

"Wasn't Ben your friend?" she asked. "Wouldn't he have let you off the hook if you told him you couldn't pay up?"

"Ben was no angel," the ranger growled. He glared at her for a long moment, then crouched down, pulled a long knife from his boot, and tossed it onto her lap. She gaped at him.

"Ben was a rat," he continued, as if nothing had happened. "I was already on a short leash at the ranger station thanks to my love for the ponies. If I didn't pay him, he would have been more than happy to tell the sheriff that I'd been up to my old habits, and I couldn't afford that. Russ is a good friend, but he's an even better cop. He would have told my boss, and I would have lost my job. I wasn't planning on killing Ben, not exactly, but when I saw him slinking around the pizzeria late at night while I was heading out to the park, I knew I had the perfect chance. Thankfully I had my personal firearm in the glove compartment. After that, it was just a matter of filing off the serial number. If it wasn't for your grandmother, I would have had no trouble planting it at your house."

"What am I supposed to do with this?" Ellie

asked, nudging the knife in her lap gingerly. The crazy thought entered her mind that he expected her to duel him.

"I can't shoot an unarmed woman," he said simply. "It would look better if you had a gun, but the knife will have to do."

He reached for the firearm holstered on his hip, undoing the snap almost casually. The gun was a sinister-looking matte black. Ellie paled.

"Please, don't do this," she begged. "I won't tell anyone; I promise…"

"Oh, shut up," he said. "I hate begging."

He unholstered the gun. "This will look better for me if you pick up the knife, you know," he said. "I can say you ambushed me, attacked me out of the blue and I had no choice but to defend myself. Go on, pick it up." He waited a moment, and when she did nothing, he sighed and aimed the gun at her. "Well, I guess it doesn't matter that much."

He placed his finger on the trigger, and Ellie squeezed her eyes shut.

"Drop the gun, Duncan!"

Her eyes snapped open. She knew that voice. It was Russell. He was approaching them slowly, his own gun drawn and pointed at his friend.

"Drop it now. I *will* shoot."

Ellie saw the muzzle of Duncan's gun waver in indecision, and she decided to take the chance while she had it. Grabbing the knife in her lap, she lunged forward and slashed it toward his leg. He let out a howl of pain and dropped the gun, staggering away from her and falling backwards over the car behind him. She watched, frozen in shock, as Russell rushed forward to handcuff his friend.

As he heaved Duncan to his feet, she noticed a spreading red stain on the sleeve of the man's jacket. It took her a moment to realize what it must be. Her grandmother had shot at the intruder, and ever since, whenever she had seen Duncan, he had been wearing long sleeves. She felt a rush of admiration for the old woman, who had managed to drive off a killer on her own even though she was in her eighties.

"I guess my grandmother didn't miss after all, did she?" she said quietly as the sheriff hauled his best friend away.

Epilogue

Eleanora straightened the stack of papers on her grandfather's—no, on *her* desk, and looked over at Marlowe, who was sitting contentedly on a wooden stand by the window. Over the past few weeks, she and the bird had developed a wary sort of mutual trust, but she knew there was still a long way to go before the macaw would view her as a friend.

"Are you ready to go back to your cage now?" she asked. Marlowe tilted her head, staring at Ellie for a long moment before slowly raising one clawed foot into the air; an imperious gesture that the woman had quickly learned meant *carry me.*

She stood up and walked slowly over to the stand. The bird stepped onto her extended arm without hesitation, then clamped down tightly as Ellie walked out of the study. Bunny rushed out in front of them, her flag-like tail raised proudly as she led the way to the cage near the stairs. Both animals were starting to get used to the new routine.

Ellie transferred the parrot to the cage, then hurried to the kitchen to wash up, smiling as she heard the bird yell *goodbye* as she walked away. The more comfortable Marlowe got with her, the more the bird seemed to say, and the macaw was turning out to have quite the vocabulary.

"This looks great, as always, Nonna," she said when she joined her grandmother at the table. "Remember, tomorrow it's my turn to cook."

"I'm elderly, I'm not a kindergartner," the old woman said. "I know how to take turns. Now dig in before it gets cold."

They chatted about small things until their plates were nearly empty, then the talk turned to business.

"How are things at the restaurant this week?"

"About the same as last week after the grand re-opening," Ellie said. "We've got about twice the number of customers we had before, and that number is holding steady. I haven't had any more complaints about pizzas getting delivered cold either, so it seems like Jacob is really turning over a new leaf."

"See? You're a natural at this," her grandmother

said. She hesitated, her eyes examining her grand-daughter's face. "And how are you feeling about what happened?"

"Having a gun shoved in my face, you mean?" Ellie looked down at her plate. She had woken up in a panic a couple of times after dreaming that she was back at the car with Duncan. "I think it will take a while to get over it completely, but for the most part I'm fine."

"You're stronger than you know, dear," the elderly woman said. "How about that sheriff? Have you spoken to him yet?"

"No," Ellie said. "I've been pretty busy."

The truth was, she had seen Russell twice since he had arrested Duncan and saved her, and both times he had given her only the most cursory of greetings. At least he had been willing to explain to her how he found her in time… and it was chilling to think that it had been nothing but chance. He had just been arriving to attend the pizzeria's grand re-opening when he had seen his best friend threatening her with a gun. She was amazed that he had been able to put his personal feelings aside and figure out what was going on in time. She supposed that what Duncan had said was true; Russell had been a good friend, but an even better cop.

The fact remained that she had been key in uncovering the fact that his friend was a murderer. She didn't blame him for resenting her, but couldn't help being disappointed. He seemed like a genuinely good guy, and she had hoped at the very least to continue a friendly relationship with him.

"Things will straighten themselves out." Her grandmother squeezed her hand reassuringly before getting up. "I'm glad you came home, Ellie. This old house sure is brighter with you around."

Ellie smiled, watching the old woman as she bustled around the kitchen. *She's right*, she thought. *This is home. Maybe it's not exactly what I wanted my middle-aged life to be like, but that doesn't mean I can't make something wonderful out of it anyway. I didn't just turn a page in my life, I opened up a whole new book. And it's up to me what sort of story it ends up being.*

***

If you enjoyed Pall Bearers and Pepperoni, check out the next book in the series, Bacon Cheddar Murder, today!

Turn the page for a sneak preview!

Eleanora Pacelli pulled open the oven and peered inside. What she saw made her smile.

"Perfect," she said, reaching for the oven mitt. "Nonna, come sit down... it's done."

She took the pizza stone out of the oven and placed it on a rack, then pulled the pizza wheel out of a drawer. Expertly, precisely, she sliced the pizza into eighths, then transferred the entire stone to a trivet on the small table in the breakfast nook. Her grandmother Ann Pacelli had already taken her seat. The old woman, with her professionally curled white hair and turquoise reading glasses, eyed the pizza critically for a moment, then beamed.

"It looks just like how your grandfather used to make it," she said. "This was always one of my favorite dinners. Sausage and tomato pizza with real mozzarella… it was the first pizza he ever made for me."

Ellie smiled, glad that she had been able to bring back good memories for the elderly woman who had done so much for her over the past few weeks. It was a good start on the long road to making up for all of the years she had neglected to visit after moving away as a teen. Twenty-five years was a long time to go without seeing someone, though, and it would take a lot more than a pizza dinner to alleviate some of the guilt she felt about it.

"Don't compliment me just yet," Ellie said, reaching for a piece. "Let's see how it tastes first."

The pizza was just about perfect. The cheese was melted and gooey, the sauce was bursting with flavor, and the crust was light and airy. In the weeks since Ellie had moved back to Kittiport, Maine, she had had a crash course on pizza making. Taking over her grandfather's pizzeria, Papa Pacelli's, hadn't been easy, but it had been rewarding—more so than any job she'd ever had. She took pride in creating some-thing with her own hands, even if that something was only a pizza.

They ate their lunch in a comfortable silence. Bunny, Ellie's little black-and-white papillon, waited eagerly under the table for dropped tidbits. Ellie had the suspicion that her grandmother was sneaking the dog little bits of sausage, but couldn't complain—she was saving her last pizza crust for Marlowe, after all.

The large parrot was hanging on the cage bars when Ellie left the kitchen after finishing lunch with her grandmother. She greeted Ellie with a loud squawk, and the woman smiled. Marlowe, a green-winged macaw, had been her grandfather's. The bird had been devastated after he passed away, and was just now beginning to show her normal, undepressed, personality. Ellie had never had a bird, and was still wary of that big, bone-colored beak, but was quickly learning just how much personality the parrot had. She was a joy to interact with.

"I've got a treat for you, Marlowe," she said as she opened the cage door. "Pizza." She held up the pizza crust, watching the bird's light gold pupils shrink to pinpricks as she recognized one of her favorite foods.

With a smile, Ellie handed her the crust. The bird held it in one clawed foot, while nibbling small pieces off with her beak.

"What do you say?" she prodded gently. Her beak full of pizza crust, Marlowe gave a garbled "thank you," and Ellie smiled. The bird was smart, that was certain. She was nineteen years old, and had been raised since she was a chick by Arthur and Ann Pacelli. She was constantly surprising Ellie by saying something new, and often what she said was in context.

"Well, I've got to go to work," the woman said. "Goodbye."

She opened the front door, paused to scratch Bunny behind the ears, and smiled when she heard the bird call "Goodbye!" after a second. Between the bird and the dog, she knew her grandmother wouldn't be lonely.

Papa Pacelli's was in downtown Kittiport, not far from the marina. The old brick building had housed the pizzeria for nearly twenty years, making the restaurant a real fixture in town. It had lost popularity over the last two years as her grandfather stepped back from managing it. The young man that he had hired as manager turned out not to be as trustworthy as he hoped. Xavier Hurst had spent his two years there stealing funds from the pizzeria, and had done little to ensure that the other employees completed their tasks. With orders often getting delivered late and cold, and the pizzeria itself falling into disrepair, the restaurant ended up losing most of its customer base.

All that changed after Ellie took over. Once she found out that Xavier had been stealing from the pizzeria, she fired him and took over as manager herself. The other employees, Rose, Jacob, and Clara, had all done much better since she had made it clear that she wouldn't allow any more fooling around at work... especially if it kept the customers waiting.

She got to the restaurant shortly before Jacob and Rose were supposed to arrive. It was a good feeling to walk into a clean and organized kitchen. She opened one fridge and smiled to see neatly organized rows of balled pizza dough on the shelves. The top two shelves had Ellie's favorite thick-crust pizza dough, and on the bottom was their dough for thin-crust pizzas. Although Ellie had grown up in Kittiport, the decades she'd spent in Chicago had made her a true lover of thick-crust pizza. She considered the thin-crust pizza much preferred by easterners to be not much better than tomato sauce on crackers. The other fridge was stocked with all sorts of vegetables, cheeses, and meats, while the pantry held dry ingredients for various sauces, as well as the flour and yeast required to make the dough. Nearly everything they served was made from scratch, something that Ellie knew her grandfather had been very proud of.

We really do make the best pizza in town, she

thought as she fired up the ovens. To be fair, there wasn't much competition… other than Cheesaroni Calzones. *I still can't believe that Jeffrey hired Xavier after I fired him. How can he trust him? It would serve him right if Xavier stole from him, too.*

She wasn't usually a vengeful person, but the owner of the calzone shop had been nothing but rude to her ever since she arrived in town. She suspected that he and Xavier had been behind the sabotage that had taken place at the pizzeria a few weeks ago—in fact, she all but knew that they were behind it—but with no evidence against them, the best she had been able to do was to change the locks and keep an eye open for any more suspicious activity from the pair of them. She had the feeling that she hadn't heard the last of them yet.

"Hi Ms. Pacelli," one of the employees said as she came in through the back entrance. "How was your weekend?"

"Pretty good, Rose. Thanks for asking. How was yours?"

"Great." The young woman grinned. "I went down to Portland with some friends. We had pizza, but it was nowhere near as good as it is here."

"I'm glad to hear that," Ellie said, smiling. "Take a moment to clock in and get settled, then will you start folding some boxes? I'm going to go unlock the front doors. Fold a few more than you usually do. If this week is anything like last week, we'll need them."

***

Ready for more?

Pick up your copy of Bacon Cheddar Murder today!

Printed in Great Britain
by Amazon

83815334R00071